ADDED S

If security is an issue,
entries — or just a few ~~select secret words~~ — in code. One way
of doing this is to create your own personal cipher wheel.

To make your cipher wheel, trace the inner and outer circles on
the next page. Transfer the circles to a piece of light card, cut
them out, then join them in the middle using a paper fastener.

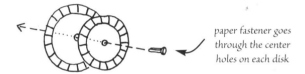

paper fastener goes
through the center
holes on each disk

Now transfer the 26 wedges onto your wheel. Fill in the letters
of the alphabet clockwise around the outer wheel. In the spaces
on the inner circle, fill in whatever you like, as long as each
letter in the alphabet on the outer wheel has a corresponding,
unique letter, number, or symbol on the inner wheel.

When you've filled in all the spaces on the inner wheel, line up
any symbol on the inner wheel with the letter A on the outer
wheel. Mark this symbol on the inner wheel to remind you that
this is your starting point.

outer circle
inner circle

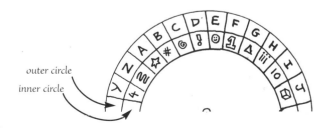

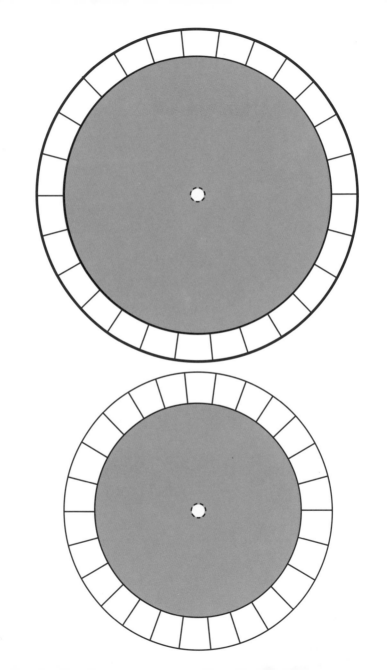

In this book...

Important Things to Know About Me

Me and My Family

My Family Roots

Where I Live

Me and My Friends

My Favorites

What's Going on in My World

Magic (and Not So Magic) Moments

Emotionally Speaking

The Inside Story

Encounters with Others

Future Announcements

This journal is divided into sections for you to fill in when the mood takes you. If you run out of space, use extra paper or a blank notebook and just keep on writing!

Writers often dedicate their books to people they look up to or are particularly fond of. Why don't you dedicate this book to someone special in your life: a parent, a grandparent, a friend who's always there for you?

I dedicate this book to

My mom and my

Grade 5 teacher

What  Look Like

Stick in recent photographs or give your best artist's impression of how you look.

Here's me on
a good day . . .

Date:

Occasion:

Here's me on
a bad day . . .

Date:

Occasion:

My **First Day** on the Planet

It's a girl!

Date _Jan 3 2013_ Time _Thursday 2:14 am_
Weight _8 lvs 8oz_ Place _VG_

What kind of baby were you? Quiet? Fussy? Smiley? Bald?
(Check with your parents to see what they remember!)

Smiley

World events in the year _____:

Family events in the year _____:

Terms of Endearment

My full name is _____

My name means _____

I'm usually called _____

WHEN MY PARENTS ARE MAD AT ME, THEY CALL ME

_____ .

Do you like your name?
Do you know why your parents chose it?

What would you rather be called and why?

When I **Was** Young

My first words were . . .

The person who taught me how to tie my

shoelaces was _____.

The person who taught me how to ride my

bike was _____.

My earliest memory:

What others remember about me:

Ask if your parents kept a baby book, or letters or tapes from when you were young. If you have older brothers or sisters, ask what they remember.

More space for memories — and photos, if you have them. (If you don't have photos, draw a picture of what you think you were like as a baby.)

Who Am I Now?

*Imagine you are stranded on a desert island with someone
you have never seen before. Your fellow castaway asks
what is the most important thing to know about you.*

The most important thing to know about me is . . .

*If you could bring only three things
with you to your desert island,
what would they be?*

Take a Moment to *Dream*

On a clear night, take a walk outside and look up at the stars.
Consider the vastness of the night sky and ask yourself:
"If I could choose a different time or place in which to be
born, what would it be and why?" If you wouldn't change
a thing, why wouldn't you?

ME

AND MY
FAMILY

The **People** I Live With

If you have photos of your family, stick them on this page. If you don't, draw or describe the people you live with. Note one special feature for everyone.

Where **i** Fit In

Are you the oldest? The youngest?
Somewhere in the middle?

Are there too many brothers and sisters in your home?
Not enough? Just the right number?

Do you have your father's smile? Your mother's temper?

What special things are there about you that
no one else in your family shares?

spotlight on **Family**

Family moments that I treasure:

Family moments that make me proud:

Your grandma really does wear army boots?

Things About My Family That
Drive **Me** Crazy

Do any members of your family have really annoying habits?
Unload your pet peeves and frustrations here.

Come back to this page when you need to vent your feelings
or just to see whether things have gotten better or worse!

Family **Activities** to Share

*Make a note of special family activities to celebrate
holidays — or any special times. Which of these
family traditions would you like to pass on?*

Family **Favorites**

*Can your brother make great lemonade? Does your aunt make
festive decorations to celebrate the summer solstice? Write
down their instructions for favorite family recipes and crafts.*

Great (and Not So Great)
Family Vacations

What are the most fun family vacations you've ever had?
Which ones really sucked? Why?

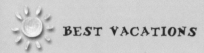

BEST VACATIONS

WORST VACATIONS

If you were responsible for planning the next family vacation, where would you go, how would you get there, and what special things would you see?

*Stick in one of your holiday photos or postcards
(or draw the scene for your fantasy vacation
postcard on the next page).*

My **Perfect** Vacation

*Write yourself a postcard from your fantasy vacation spot.
It doesn't have to be anywhere that really exists —
or maybe it does exist and you just don't know about it yet!*

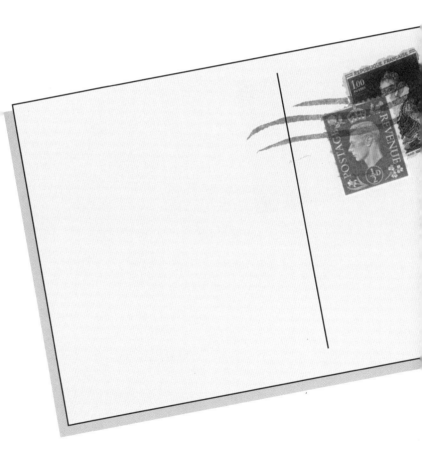

Pets, **Glorious** Pets

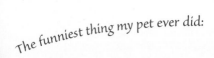

(If you have no pets, borrow one of your friends' pets to help you fill out this page!)

My pet is

My pet has the following peculiar habits:

The funniest thing my pet ever did:

The best thing about my pet is

Fill this space with doodles and photos, or poems about your favorite pet(s) or the pet(s) you would like to have. If you got a pet tomorrow, what kind of animal would it be and what would you call it?

Take a Moment to Dream

Before falling asleep one night, ask yourself if you have ever wished your family were different and why. When you wake up in the morning — before you do anything else — bring this journal under the covers with you and jot down your answer here.

MY
FAMILY
ROOTS

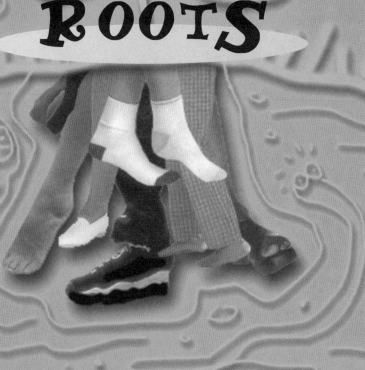

My Family Tree

Draw as much of your family tree as you know across these two pages. Fill in your relatives' names and, if you can find out, when they were born and died, and what they did in their lives. Call your grandma or grandpa to find out more.

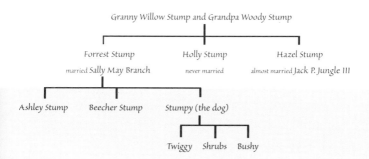

Granny Willow Stump and Grandpa Woody Stump

Forrest Stump
married Sally May Branch

Holly Stump
never married

Hazel Stump
almost married Jack P. Jungle III

Ashley Stump

Beecher Stump

Stumpy (the dog)

Twiggy   Shrubs   Bushy

My Family

Draw or stick in a map and mark the places where people in your family have lived or where different members of your family live now. Make your map as plain or fancy, as accurate or rough, as you like. (Think of treasure maps, street maps, satellite images, or maps of the world.)

N

Where My Family Comes From

How did your family come to where you live now? If your family hasn't always lived in this country, where did they come from? If you feel inspired, write up your family history as a newspaper article under a snappy headline.

MARS?

Update this page as you learn more about your family's past.

Extra! Extra!

A page for late-breaking family news.

FAMILY WEEKLY

AUNT RUTH GROWS A BEARD

"One day she woke up and it was just there!" Blah blah blah blah blah blahblah blah blah blah blahblah blah blah blah blahblah blah blah blah blahblah blah blah blah blah blahblah blah blah blah blahblah blah blah blah blah blahblah blah blah blah blah blahblah blah blah blah blah

blah blah blah blah blahblah blah blah blah blahblah blah blah blah blah blahblah blah blah blah blah blah blah- blah blah blah blah blah blahblah blah blah blah blahblah blah blah blah blah blahblah blah blah blah blah

blah blah blah blah blahblah blah blah blah blahblah blah blah blah blah blahblah blah blah blah blah blahblah blah blah blah blah blahblah blah blah blah blah blahblah blah blah blah blah blah blah blah blahblah blah blah blah blah blah blahblah blah b blahblah blah b blahblah blah b blah blahblah blah blah blah blah blah blah blahblah blah blah blahblah blah blah blahblah blahblah blah blahblah blah blah blahblah

Take a Moment to *Dream*

Imagine waking up one morning and not remembering anything about who you are or where you come from. If this happened to you and you could invent a new past for yourself or your family, what would you say?

WHERE I LIVE

My **Home**

My address is _____

_____

_____

This has been my home since I was _____ years old.

PLACES I LIVED BEFORE:

*Imagine who might have lived in your home
before you. What do you think they were like?*

Stick in a photograph of your home, draw a picture of it, or sketch out a floor plan. Mark places in and around your home that are important to you.

My  Room

My room is *MESSY* / **NEAT** (circle one).

I clean it _____ times a _____.

My mother would like me to clean it
more / less (circle one) often.

*What do you like to do or keep in
your room? What are you not
allowed to do or keep in your room?*

*Can you shut the door and keep
other people out? Would you like to?*

*Do you ever bring food up to your
room and then forget about it?*

Draw a plan of your room, or set your imagination free and draw your dream room.

My Special Place
in My Neighborhood

*Describe your favorite place near where you live. It doesn't
need to be a big place, like a store or a park. It could be a
small place, like a doorstep to sit on or a corner where you
meet your friends. If you don't have a special place,
why not make one up?*

Draw your real or imagined special place (or find a picture of it and stick it here). Label the features that make this place so special.

Take a Moment to Dream

Take a long, hot bath, put on something comfortable, and curl up somewhere snug and warm. Then think, if you could choose where to live, what kind of home would you want? Would it be big and grand or small and cozy? Would it be in the city or out in the country? Would it be a castle, a farm house, or a fancy apartment? Describe your dream home in words and pictures.

pic of me

ME

AND MY
FRIENDS

My

List your friends here. What are they like
(best points/worst points)? How long have you
known them? How did you get to be friends?

What do you have in common with your friends?

What makes them different from you?

Do you want to be more like them or less like them?

Getting  It

Has a friend ever hurt your feelings?

What did you do to get over it?

Would you do that again or would
you do something different?

The  **Meanest** Thing I Ever Did

*What's the meanest thing you ever
did to one of your friends?*

DID YOU MAKE UP FOR IT?

What would you do if you found yourself in that situation again?

The **Nicest** Thing I Ever Did

What's the nicest thing you ever did for a friend?

How did your friend react?

Would you do that again?

personality **Quiz**

*Try this personality quiz just for fun! Using the table
at the end of this quiz, rank your answers to each
question from 4 to 1, with 4 being the most like you
and 1 being the least like you.*

1. *What do you like doing most?*

A. Meeting new people
B. Getting through your to-do list
C. Perfecting your latest innovative idea
D. Getting out there and being active

2. *When you work on a team project
at school, what concerns you most?*

A. That everyone works together
B. That everyone understands what's expected of them
C. That the results are significant
D. That you do things a little differently from
   everyone else

3. *Which of these descriptions fits you best?*

A. A caring person
B. A dependable person
C. A curious person
D. An adventurous person

4. Which of these people do you
see yourself as being most like?

A. The person people come to when they need to talk
B. The person people come to when they need help
solving a problem
C. The person people come to when they need an
opinion on a complicated matter
D. The person people come to when they need to
forget their worries

5. Do you like to be

A. Relaxed?
B. Organized?
C. Private?
D. Busy?

6. What's most important to you?

A. Getting along with people
B. Following the rules
C. Seeking out challenges
D. Keeping things interesting and fun

Total your scores here.

Q.	1	2	3	4	5	6	TOTAL
A			A		A	A	3
B				B			1
C							
D	D	D					2

You may score higher in one category than in another, or you may find that your scores are fairly evenly distributed across the four personality types. Turn the page to learn more about the defining characteristics of A, B, C, and D types.

A types are sensitive people who like to be in tune with the people around them. They like creative tasks where they can interact with others. They are thoughtful and relaxed. A types often become counselors, teachers, or writers.

B types are responsible people who work hard. They like structured environments where the rules are clear. They are conscientious and dependable. B types often become administrators, doctors, or lawyers.

C types are problem-solvers who are often perfectionists. They like to work on their own to develop new ideas. They are independent and thrive on challenge. C types often become scientists, engineers, or judges.

D types are spontaneous people who seek out adventure. They like flexibility and variety, and they handle crises well. They are competitive and charming. D types often become athletes, artists, or marketing whizzes.

 Hanging Out

What do you do when you get together with your friends?
Give five stars for the best times, four stars for the next
best, and so on. (Half stars are allowed!)

Yahoo!

My **Personal** Yearbook

Stick photos of your friends here, with notes about what makes them special.

space for more notes and pictures

Hope all your dreams come true

Take a Moment to Dream

Take this journal to a park or quiet space near your home. Sit on a bench or under a tree and write down all the things that make a good friend.

MY
FAVORITES

Movie Favorites

What are your favorite movies? Did they make you laugh out loud? Reach for the box of tissues? Bite your nails?

MOVIE : harry poter

MY MINI-REVIEW :

Bite my nails

MOVIE : the gide to monster hunting

MY MINI-REVIEW :

laugh

MOVIE : Luca

MY MINI-REVIEW :

laugh

My Movie

If you were in charge of making a movie, which actors would you cast and what roles would they play?

Would you cast yourself in a leading role? Bit part? Not at all?

What would be the plot of your movie?

Music for My Mood

The best music for daydreaming is

The best music for singing along out loud is

The best music to accompany homework is

The best music to dance to is

Favorite **Bands** and **Artists**

List your favorite bands or artists. Why do you like them? Is it because they sing about things that have happened to you? You really like the way they look? You can't get their music out of your head?

I LIKE . . .   **BECAUSE . . .**

Favorite **Books**
When I Was Young

What books did you read or did someone
read to you when you were young?

Which characters were most frightening?

Which characters were most lovable?

Which stories were most exciting?

Hickory, Dickory, Dock.

Favorite Books **Today**

My favorite authors:

My favorite series:

Fill in any of the following that apply to you.

A book that made me want to fix what's wrong with the world:

A book that showed me how wonderful people can be:

A book that took me to places I'd never been:

A book that taught me stuff I never knew:

A book I read when I wanted to escape:

Favorite, Fabulous **Clothes**

Describe or draw your favorite outfit —
or create an original design.

Tie

Favorite, Fabulous **Hair**

Draw your hairstyle and experiment with different styles: for volleyball tournaments, camping BBQ's, yachting holidays, attending the Oscars, bathing the dog.

Record the worst haircut you ever had here:

_____

_____

_____

_____

Hello! We need hair too!

Collections of Favorite **Things**

You've probably collected something at some time in your life: coins, Beanie babies, hippopotamuses. Record your best-ever collection here.

NAME OF COLLECTION:

DATE STARTED:

DESCRIPTION:

WHAT HAPPENED?

My **Scrapbook**
of Really Cool Stuff

*Cut out pictures from magazines or
download images from the Internet to make a
collage of really cool stuff — favorite flowers,
best lipstick colors, neat products.*

More cool stuff. . .

WHAT'S GOING ON IN MY WORLD

My **Life Line**

Mark important events in your life along this timeline.
Include dates if you can remember them.

START

← I was born!

More of my life line ...

WHERE I am Now!

My **School Report** Card

*Rate your school and see how close it comes
to meeting YOUR expectations.*

Name of school: _____
Name of principal: _____
My grade: _____

Subject: _____
Teacher: _____
School's performance: Not even close / Getting there / Cool / Excellent!
Comments:

Subject: _____
Teacher: _____
School's performance: Not even close / Getting there / Cool / Excellent!
Comments:

Subject: _____
Teacher: _____
School's performance: Not even close / Getting there / Cool / Excellent!
Comments:

Subject: _____
Teacher: _____
School's performance: Not even close / Getting there / Cool / Excellent!
Comments:

Subject: _____
Teacher: _____
School's performance: Not even close / Getting there / Cool / Excellent!
Comments:

So, does your school get a passing or a failing grade?

Areas of strength:

Areas needing improvement:

Overall assessment:

Final mark:

The **Things** That I Do

What are your special talents? Do you like to draw, skateboard, write? Do you take music lessons? Learn martial arts? Play sports?

What's your favorite activity? How did you come to choose it? Is it something you hope to keep doing for a long time?

My Achievement Log

Use this page to record your competition
results, team scores, or personal bests.

Contributions **and** Earnings

*Do you have a part-time job? Walk the dog?
Volunteer? List your chores or jobs, the amount
of time you spend at them, and what, if anything,
you get in return (an allowance, a wage, the
satisfaction of a job well done).*

Fast Food

Odd Jobs

Babysitting

Maximum **Relaxation**

When you get stressed out, what do you do? Do you
shut your bedroom door and crank up the music?
Pick up the phone and talk the ear off your best friend?

My favorite place to go when I feel stressed out is

What I do to relax:

The person who's best at calming me down:

Ahhhhhhhh

Take a Moment to *Dream*

Do you sometimes feel you have too much going on in your life? Not enough? Some evening when the table is cleared and your homework's done, make a plan for how you'd like your week to unfold. Base it on your real life — or go wild and draw up a timetable for the life you'd rather be leading!

Express yourself on these two pages — whether you feel like screaming at your mother or snuggling into your favorite chair to daydream. Experiment with words written in different colors and bordered by different shapes to capture the variety of your emotions.

Match some of your feelings to the events that triggered them. (For instance, "Furious with sister — wore my new boots without asking.")

My  Fears

Are you afraid of enclosed spaces, spiders, monsters lurking in the dark? You might be afraid of being hit or having your feelings hurt — or of hurting others. Explore your fears here.

Think of at least four words that describe how you feel when you're afraid:

Uh! Oh!

My list of fears:

shots

Have you found any ways of getting rid of mild jitters or blind panic? Perhaps your friends have ideas? Write down your ideas and put a checkmark by them if they work.

Five ideas about what to do in the face of fear:

Things I used to be afraid of when I was little:

WHAT?
I'm just a friendly
little BAT!

My

To worry is to suffer from a nagging feeling of uneasiness.
We all worry about things — big things and little things.

THINGS I USED TO WORRY ABOUT WHEN I WAS LITTLE:

What do you worry about now? Getting zits? War in far-off countries? Unload your worries by writing them down here.

MY PERSONAL LIST OF WORRIES:

Think of how you might worry less. If you get a chance to try your solution, note whether it worked or not.

IDEAS ABOUT WHAT TO DO
IN THE FACE OF WORRY:

ARE THERE TIMES WHEN
IT'S GOOD TO WORRY?

My **Bug** Page

Do you hate the disgusting way Auntie May picks her teeth after eating corn? Does one of your friends always keep the rest of you waiting?

When something really bugs me, I feel like

What can you do about the incredibly annoying
things other people do? Try the following chart.
Note what bugs you and mark what action you can
take: avoid the situation [!], change the situation [O],
or change your reaction to the situation [∾].

It really bugs me when...

SITUATION	ACTION	HOW DID I DO?

My **Reprogramming** Page

Your feelings and how you act on them affect the world around you. Here's an exercise to try if you'd like to get a grip on feelings and their consequences.

STEP 1: Reprogram the voice inside your head

- Take a piece of paper and imagine yourself back in a particularly swampy period in your life. As you relive the experience, ask yourself:

  - How unbearable is this?
  - What thoughts or beliefs inside my head are making me feel that way?

- When you know what that little voice inside your head is saying, ask yourself:

  - Are my thoughts and beliefs true? (For instance, do they really all hate me, or is it just that blond guy at the back of the class?)

● *If you suspect your thoughts or beliefs may not be true, ask yourself:*

- Am I blowing things way out of proportion?
- Am I expecting things to always turn out the way I want them to?
- Am I underestimating my ability to handle the situation?

What do you think about the little voice in your head now? If it had given you a different message, would you have felt differently?

STEP 2: *Rate your reactions*

● *You have the power to react differently to situations too. Some reactions are more helpful than others. Think about your reaction and ask yourself:*

- Did my reaction harm or help anyone?
- Did my reaction bring out the best in me and others?
- Did my reaction help me get closer to my goal?
- Did my reaction help me to be the kind of person I want to be?

My Personal **Power** Page

Sometimes life is really tough.
Where do you find the strength to cope?

Where I find strength inside me:

People who give me power:

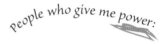

People I can talk to or just be with:

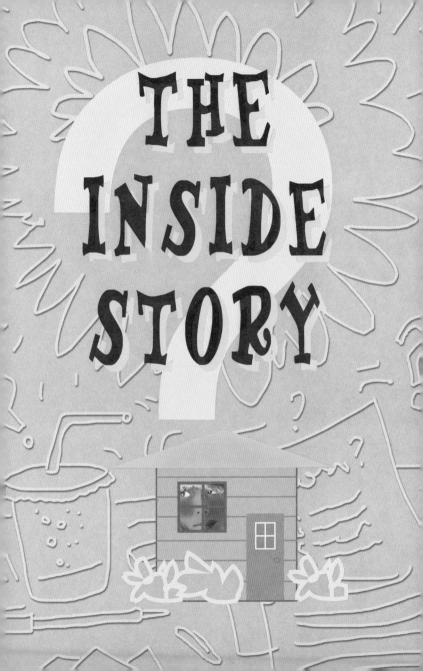

THE INSIDE STORY

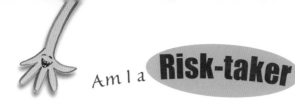 Am I a **Risk-taker**

What risks have you taken lately? How did they feel?
Would you take them again? (You can list physical risks,
like bungee jumping, or emotional risks, like phoning
a boy you like.)

Which risks did you not take and now wish you had?

Am I a Leader or a Follower?

Some people like to take charge and tell other people what to do. Others prefer to go along with the group. Answer these questions to find out where you fit in.

When I'm with friends, who decides what we're going to do? _Me_

When the whole class has to make a decision, do I get actively involved? _Sometimes_

When I'm at home, do I organize activities for my family? _Yes & No_

What leadership qualities do I have?

What qualities make me a good follower?

Am I a **Loner**?

Some people are happiest curled up with a book. Others like nothing better than the hype of the crowd at a football game. Where do you feel most at home?

I'M HAPPIEST WHEN:

* I'm on my own

* I'm with my family

* I'm with a group of friends

* I'm with my best friend

MY FAVORITE THING TO DO WHEN I'M ON MY OWN IS

Am I a **Procrastinator**?

Procrastinators are people who put things off until tomorrow. Think of the past month. List tasks you completed ahead of schedule, tasks you got done just in time, and any deadlines you completely blew.

Tasks Completed Ahead of Schedule

1 _____

2 _____

3 _____

Tasks Completed Just in Time

1 _____

2 _____

3 _____

Missed Deadlines

1 _____

2 _____

Do you think you have a problem with

time management? _____

Would your mother/homeroom teacher agree? _____

How **Inquisitive** Am I ?

What do you wonder about? Come back to this space from time to time to see if you know more now than you did then.

I'd like to know why

I'd like to know if it's true that

I'd like to know what would happen if

How **Competitive** Am I?

For some people, everything they do is a competition. Other people prefer to follow their own interests no matter what others are doing. Answer these questions to rate your competitive side.

I prefer team sports _____
I prefer individual sports _____

I hate it when my team loses _____
I play sports for fun _____

I enter competitions whenever I can _____
I try to avoid evaluations of any sort _____

I do my best work on a strict schedule _____
I like working at my own pace _____

I like to win at everything I do _____
I do things because they interest me _____

How **Easily Influenced** Am I ?

It can be hard to know when to listen to others, and when to listen to yourself. What would you do in these situations?

You wear an outfit you think looks great on you, but your friends give it the thumbs down. Do you change it? _____

One of the most popular boys in class has an idea for a prank that makes you uneasy. Do you go along with it anyway? _____

Your father tells you you'll never make a sports team, but you think you can. Do you insist on trying out anyway? _____

Write about a recent dilemma when you had to decide whether to trust the judgments of others or your own instincts.

How Comfortable Am I with **Change** ?

What changes have you been through lately? Maybe your best friend moved away, or your grandfather moved in, or your mother got a new job. Write the event in the middle of the page and circle it. Then write words to describe how you felt, coming out from the circle like rays from the sun.

I don't like being upside down.

More About **Change**

Thinking back over the years, what has been a bad change in your life? Did it feel like a bad change at the time? Do you see it differently now?

What has been a good change in your life? Did it feel like a good change at the time? Do you see it differently now?

List five ways YOU'VE changed in the past year, big or small.

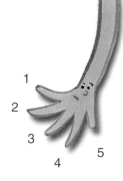

1

2

3

4

5

A Page to Celebrate Me

Not everything in life always needs changing! Write down all the reasons you like yourself just the way you are.

 ME ME ME ME ME ME ME ME ME!

ENCOUNTERS

WITH

OTHERS

Likes **and** Dislikes

People are so different. Think of aggressive people, courageous people, kind people, funny people, thoughtful people. What qualities do you like and dislike?

I like her...
I like her not!...

I like people who are

I don't like people who are

Think about the qualities you dislike. Why don't you like them?

Disappointments **and** Surprises

Were you ever counting on someone who didn't come through? Did it ever turn out that someone was not who you thought they were?

Has anyone ever turned out to be much nicer than you expected? Perhaps you didn't much like them at first, but then something made you change your mind?

Inspirations

Think of family, friends, characters in real life or in books or movies who have shown you that individuals can make a difference. List them here. What is it that makes them so special?

These are all people who make me look at life in a different way.

Reaching **Out**

Has anyone ever come to you for help? A friend? Your little brother? List things you've done to help people and what it is about you that means you were able to help in this way.

Take a Moment to Dream

If time and money were no object, who would you most want to help and why? (You could think of a global problem, an issue in your neighborhood or school, or someone in your family who could use some support.)

FUTURE

ANNOUNCEMENTS

The **World** Is Waiting

List places you'd like to go and what you'd like
to do there. These can be places for the mind,
body, heart, or soul (or all of the above).

Let's **GO!**

Do you want to — search out your family's roots, learn a new language, climb a m

My Fantastic **Career**

List your requirements for an ideal job.
(For instance, late start, plenty of fresh air, free parking.)

List (or invent!) jobs that meet these requirements.

Can you think of ways you might prepare
for any of the jobs you listed?

My Lifetime **Achievement** Award !!!

A hush falls over the audience as you step into the spotlight to receive an award to celebrate your life. What would you like this award to be for? Design your certificate, plaque, or trophy here.

My Ideal Partner

Think of the perfect person for you. On the left, list qualities this lucky person will have. In the second column, list qualities you have. Use one color to highlight the qualities that are the same and a different color for those that are different.

MY IDEAL PARTNER   **ME**

Check your columns. Do you want a partner who is the same as or different from you?

That'll Be **Me**

Forget the siren call of TV teens, your little sister's views on how your personality could do with a serious overhaul, and your teachers' comments on your work ethic ("If only she would apply herself...").

What aspect of your inner self would YOU like to work on?

Visions for the  Future

Draw or describe some things you plan to include in
your life — perhaps a sailboat or a cottage, a smart red
sports car, or lots of good-looking guys. You might put
them in order of importance or in the order you plan
to have them enter your life!

What dreams are you going to keep on dreaming, no matter what?

Proud Moments

Draw yourself a ribbon, plaque, or certificate to celebrate an achievement you're especially proud of. This could be for perseverance in the face of adversity (like not arguing with your brother even though you're really mad at him) or for finishing something that was really hard for you.

The **Best** Experience of My Life

Describe the most wonderful thing that ever happened to you and how it made you feel.

The **Worst** Experience of My Life

Describe the absolutely worst thing that ever happened to you and how it made you feel.

Biggest Regrets

All of us have done things we wish we hadn't.
Record your biggest regrets here. If there are any you
think you can fix, note what you would like
to do about them.

Hmmmmmmm...

The Worst **Trouble** I Ever Got Into

What's the worst thing you ever did and got found out? Whose idea was it? What were the consequences? Would you ever do that again?

What's the worst thing you ever did and didn't get found out? Whose idea was it? Were there any consequences? Would you ever do that again?

Can you think of something that would have been even worse?

How did you handle it?

Oh dear!
Pardon me?

Burp!

What's the most
embarrassing thing that
ever happened to you!

My Most **Embarrassing** Moment

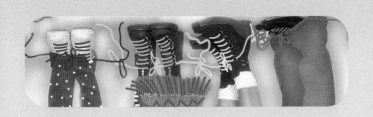

The **Funniest** Thing
That Ever Happened to Me...

What's the funniest thing that ever happened to you?

What's the best April Fool's (or other) joke you ever played on someone or someone played on you?

MAGIC
(AND NOT SO MAGIC)
MOMENTS